THIS BOOK BELONGS TO

_____

The Adventures of
Bella & Harry
Let's Visit Beijing!

Written by
Lisa Manzione

Illustrated by
Kristine Lucco

Bella & Harry, LLC

"**Come** on, Harry! Our family is boarding the chairlift that is taking us to the top of the 'Great Wall of China,' just outside the city of Beijing."

"Wow! Look, Harry! We have a great view of the wall from our chairlift."

"That is a really, really long wall, Bella!"

"Yes, it is very long! People started building the wall many, many hundreds of years ago, and then different dynasties (or families of rulers) continued to make it bigger. The wall was built to protect the people that lived in China. The part of the wall built by the Ming dynasty is more than 5,500 miles long, and the Beijing part of the wall is more than 300 miles long. Today it is one of the most visited sights in China."

The Ming dynasty portion of the Great Wall has 723 beacon towers, 7,062 lookout towers, and 3,357 wall platforms.

"**Let's** play hide and seek, Bella! You are it!"

Harry took off running along the top of the Great Wall and up the stairs to one of the many towers along the wall.

Bella knew exactly where to find Harry.

Bella was sure he was hiding in the closest tower.

"Ha! Ha! I found you! This is a lot of fun, Harry, but we are heading back to Beijing now. I will race you to the toboggan (sled)!"

"Toboggan? Bella, I thought we could only use the toboggan in the snow."

GO

BRAKE

"**Yes**, the toboggan Harry! Here at the Mutianyu portion of the Great Wall, a toboggan track has been built so we can have a fun ride down the hill. Since you are a puppy, Harry, I will drive and you can ride with me. We will follow our family . . . very slowly, Harry!"

Harry quickly ran past Bella to the toboggan. He was first in line. Off he went!

"Harry! Harry! Wait for me!" Bella yelled.

Swish! Swish! Harry picked up speed and squealed with delight as he went down the toboggan track made of metal. He was having a great time!

About four minutes later, Bella arrived at the bottom of the toboggan track.

"Harry! Harry! I told you to wait for me!"

"Let's go, Harry. We are driving back to Beijing now, but first we are going to stop at the Summer Palace."

SUMMER PALACE

"Bella, who lives in the Summer Palace?"

14

"**No** one lives in the palace now. Many years ago, the emperor (ruler)
lived in the palace. The palace has beautiful gardens, halls, temples, and lakes.
The Summer Palace was originally named the Garden of Clear Ripples."

"**Look** at all of
the interesting designs
along the Long Gallery
(or Long Corridor)."

16

"**Harry,** just think, emperors walked along the same path as we are now, enjoying the beautiful view of Kunming Lake. The Summer Palace is the largest and most cared for royal park in China."

17

"We are leaving the Summer Palace now and heading to the Temple of Heaven, which is located in the southern part of Beijing. But first, I think we are going to stop for a snack of 'sweet ears'!"

"EARS? Bella, I don't want to eat ears!!!"

18

"**Ha! Ha!** Harry, we are not going to eat real ears. The snack is called sweet ears because of the shape. Sweet ears, or 'tang er duo,' are fried cakes made with flour and sugar. They are served cold and taste very sweet. They are also very soft."

"I see the Temple of Heaven complex! How beautiful! Harry, look at the pretty blue tiles on the roof. This color blue is supposed to represent heaven."

"Bella, what was this place used for?"

"**It** was a religious temple complex with three main buildings: the Hall of Prayer for Good Harvests, the Imperial Vault of Heaven, and the Circular Mound Altar. Long ago, the emperors would come to the Temple of Heaven to worship the god of heaven and pray for a good harvest. Today, the temple complex and area around it is a park."

"**Many** people come to the park to enjoy free time together. Harry, look, some people are playing Chinese chess and others are exercising and practicing tai chi."

"Tai chi?"

22

"**Yes,** Harry . . . tai chi. Today tai chi is a form of exercise, but it started as a type of self defense. You must move very slowly and breathe deeply. Let's try it, Harry!"

Harry smiled from ear to ear. He thought tai chi was so much fun!

"Harry, our family is hungry after practicing tai chi. We are going to stop at a small restaurant and try two of the local dishes . . . Peking Duck and zha jiang mian (noodles with minced pork, vegetables, and a special sauce)."

25

"Next stop . . . the 'Forbidden City'!"

"Oh, Bella, we can't go there if it's forbidden!"

"Anyone can visit now, Harry, because the grounds and all of the buildings are a museum. When the emperor lived here, the local people were forbidden to enter the city. That is why it was called the Forbidden City. Today, the Forbidden City is known as the Palace Museum. It is the largest palace complex in the world!"

"**The** Forbidden City is divided into two sections: the northern section (Inner Court) and the southern section (Outer Court). The Inner Court is where the emperor lived with his family and the Outer Court is where the emperor worked. In total, 24 emperors lived in the Forbidden City when they were in charge of the country."

"**We** are entering through the Gate of Heavenly Peace. We will cross the square and enter the palace through the main entrance, the Meridian Gate. There are 980 buildings in the city, Harry. We will then exit through the Gate of Divine Might."

"**Bella,** why are the roofs yellow?"

世界人民 大团结万岁

"Yellow is the symbol of the royal family, so the tiles are glazed with a yellow color."

29

"Bella, look at the cool designs on the corners of the roofs. What do those animals mean?"

"Harry, the animals you see are part of the imperial roof design. The more important a building is, the more animals it will have on the roof."

Mongolia

Beijing

Japan

Yellow
Sea

CHINA

East
China Sea

Philippines

India

Bay of
Bengal

As we leave Beijing, let's take a look at our map. See, here is Beijing! China is a very large country and there is so much more to see. I know we will return, but for now it is good-bye, or zàijiàn in Chinese (Mandarin), from Bella Boo and Harry too!

Our Adventures in China

Bella attending the flag raising ceremony at Tiananmen Square.

Bella and Harry visiting the Chengdu Research Base of Giant Panda Breeding in Chengdu, China.

Harry posing with a Terracotta Warrior statue while visiting the Museum of Qin Terracotta Warriors and Horses (or the Emperor Qin Shi Huang Mausoleum Museum) in Xi'an, China.

Bella and Harry visiting the Leshan Giant Buddha near the city of Leshan, located in the Sichuan province of China.

Common Chinese (Mandarin) Phrases

Hello – Nǐ hǎo

Good-bye – Zàijiàn

Thank you – Xièxie nǐ

You're welcome – Búyòng kèqí

Please – Qǐng

Yes – Shí

No – Búshí

Good morning – Zǎo'ān

Good evening – Wǎnshang hǎo

Requests for permission to make copies of any part of the work should be directed to BellaAndHarryGo@aol.com or 855-235-5211.

Library of Congress Cataloging-in-Publications Data is available

Manzione, Lisa

The Adventures of Bella & Harry: Let's Visit Beijing!

ISBN: 978-1-937616-56-4

First Edition

Book Sixteen of Bella & Harry Series

For further information please visit:

BellaAndHarry.com

or

Email: BellaAndHarryGo@aol.com

Printed in the United States of America

Phoenix Color, Hagerstown, Maryland

March 2015

15 3 16 PC 1 1